The Roquefort Gang

Weekly Reader Books presents

The Roquefort Gang

written & illustrated by
SANDY CLIFFORD

Parnassus Press Oakland California
Houghton Mifflin Company Boston 1981

for David

This book is a presentation of
Weekly Reader Books.

Weekly Reader Books offers book clubs for children
from preschool through junior high school.
All quality hardcover books are selected by
a distinguished Weekly Reader Selection Board.

For further information write to:
Weekly Reader Books
1250 Fairwood Ave.
Columbus, Ohio 43216

Library of Congress Cataloging in Publication Data

Clifford, Sandy.
    The Roquefort Gang.

    SUMMARY: A bold trio of mice help Nicole make a
daring rescue of her two charges and the other mice held
captive in a dreadful prison.
    [1. Mice—Fiction] I. Title.
PZ7.C62226R   [Fic]   80-20269
ISBN 0-395-29521-1 (Houghton Mifflin)

❧ Contents

I ❧ NICOLE

She stood a little over two inches tall (about average for a mouse her age) with large dark brown eyes and beautiful golden brown fur. She wore a simple green and blue plaid coat and a colorful bag hung by a red cord from her shoulder. She had made the bag herself from patches of cloth and string found on the street. Nicole was proud of the bag and received many compliments whenever she wore it.

Her home was a loft above a French bakery in the middle of the city. This suited her as she was from France herself, having arrived several months earlier. The bakery, named *La Petite Souris*, stood next door to a delicatessen that featured a fine selection of cheeses from around the world. Nicole did most of her shopping at these two stores. She would usually make her purchases at night after the shops had closed and the shopkeepers had gone home. It was much easier to make her selections that way. By climbing out of the loft through a small window and running along the top of the store sign, she could then leap onto the red and blue striped awning below, and let herself into the bakery through a transom above the door that was always left open just a crack. After selecting the freshest croissant or the flakiest butter cookie, she would reach into her bag for just the right piece of bright string, shiny bottle cap, or colored stone to leave as payment. She was an honest mouse and wouldn't dream of taking something without leaving something in return.

Once, for Major Tybo's birthday party, she bought a slice of magnificent dark chocolate torte covered with bright green sprinkles. She paid for it with an elegant crystal button that reflected rainbow colors when held in the sunlight. The torte was so delicious, and made the party such a grand success, that afterwards Nicole ran back down to the bakery and added an orange movie-ticket stub next to the crystal button, calling to the deserted kitchen, *"Mes compliments au chef!"*

Nicole shared the loft with old Major Tybo and the twins. The major, who had retired years ago from the Royal Danish Mouse Corps, loved to tell stories of his military days. He told of when he was a young soldier in the famous Gruyère Wars and of when, years later while still in France, he worked secretly as cat-watch in the legendary Marseilles Cheese Underground. But that was many years ago. He was no longer young, and now it was all he could do to take care of himself and the twins. So it was very fortunate that one day, while down at the docks watching the big ships come in, he and the twins happened to meet a young French mouse who had just come off a freighter that morning. As mice always help each other in an emergency, the major offered to let Nicole stay at the loft until she could find a place of her own.

Nicole and the twins hit it off right away. They asked her hundreds of questions about France and the voyage over, and then told her of the exciting things going on in the city. They were up all night laughing and singing French peasant songs. Even the Major admitted that he hadn't had such a good time since the last Royal Danish Mouse Corps Reunion.

The twins begged Nicole to stay with them in the loft. And even the major thought it an excellent idea. In his most official-sounding voice he announced that it would be a definite boost in morale to have her as a member of the household. Nicole was delighted. All at once she had a lovely home, with a room of her own, and new friends to help keep her from getting homesick.

Nicole took it upon herself to cook breakfast each morning, then to dress the twins and take them to the park. Once there, Mrs. Applejohn, a plump motherly mouse with gray fur and pink eyes, would keep an eye on the twins while Nicole went off in search of string, buttons, stones, wrappers; any bright, colorful object that could be used in trade for food.

❦ ❦ ❦

On this particular day she had just pulled loose a length of red yarn that had been snagged in a sidewalk crack. It was just the color she needed to replace a worn-out spot of trim on Major Tybo's old military uniform.

As she put it into her bag, the sky clouded over and became dark. A drop of rain hit the pavement beside her. Then another. And another. Nicole started running back to the park. She had to get the twins home before they became drenched and caught cold. She kept close to the buildings as she ran, so as not to be stepped on by people walking along the busy sidewalk.

She arrived at the park, wet and out of breath. She saw Mrs. Applejohn leading her young son Rupert by the sleeve. Rupert was trying to step in every puddle he could reach

as his mother tugged him along.

"Where are the twins?" asked Nicole.

Mrs. Applejohn looked surprised. "The twins? ... Why ... I thought ... aren't they with ... I'm terribly sorry, dear. I'm afraid I was talking with Mrs. Orielle about the up-coming social at the Sewing Guild and ..." Mrs. Applejohn looked bewildered as she turned in every direction for a clue to where the twins might be. She perked up. "Maybe they ran home when the rain started! They're a couple of smart ones, those two. They must have run home!"

Rupert was pulling his mother in all direc-tions in his effort to leave no puddle un-stomped. "Rupert, stop that! I'm sure they ran home, dear," she shouted, trying to lead little Rupert through the wet street. "They'll be waiting, high and dry. You can count on it! Rupert, behave! A couple of smart ones, those two! Ta-ta, dear ... Rupert! I'm warn-ing you ..." Her voice trailed off as she dragged the young mouse toward their home in the rear of a café across the street.

Nicole was left standing in the street. A rumbling truck chased her to the curb and sent a splash of water over her. Soaked, she ran back to the park to look for the twins. She called their names again and again but got no answer. She turned toward home.

The rain was really coming down now and Nicole prayed she would find the twins when she got to the loft. She decided to climb up the telephone pole and take the wire; it would be much quicker in this weather. She ran from pole to pole along the thick black cable. The rain was still pouring and an occasional gust of wind forced Nicole to stop and grab tightly around the wire until it was safe to go on. At last the loft was in sight. She ran down a skinny wire that led to the little window. She crawled through the window into the loft.

Major Tybo was snoring in his rocking chair. His large belly, covered by a pink and blue quilt, rose up and down as he breathed. Nicole decided not to wake him. She took off her coat and bag and set them by the stove to dry. Then she went from room to room looking for a sign of the twins. But there was no sign. No coats. No hats. No twins.

The city is a dangerous place for a full-grown mouse let alone two little mice not much older than babies. The only thing left for Nicole to do was to go out again and look for them. She went to the kitchen, chopped off a small piece of cheese, and tore off the end of a croissant roll. She placed these in her bag which, along with her plaid coat, was beginning to dry. Then she packed as much string as she could stuff into her bag; one could never tell when one might need string in an emergency. And besides, she just might have to buy more food along the way.

Now she must leave a note for Major Tybo. She went to the desk, took out a piece of paper and a feather pen, and began to write:

Dear Major,
   You were sleeping so peacefully we decided not to wake you. The twins and I have been invited to spend the evening at Mrs. Applejohn's. You will find dinner in the bread box. Don't forget your tea.
                    love,
                    Nicole

She hated to lie about being invited to Mrs. Applejohn's but the major was much too excitable to be told what had really happened. Besides, maybe the twins were safe, hiding under a leaf somewhere nearby, waiting for the rain to stop. Then the major would have gotten all worked up for nothing. She left the note on the table next to his pipe where he would be sure to see it. She took a long red scarf and wrapped it around her neck. She put on her coat, hung her bag over her shoulder, went to the window, and slipped out silently.

8% 8% 8%

The rain had stopped as suddenly as it had started but dark clouds still filled the sky. Nicole pulled her coat tightly around her and checked to see that her bag was secure. Then she ran along the bakery sign, jumped onto the awning below, and scampered down the drainpipe to the sidewalk. Her eyes searched for the twins as she ran over the sidewalk, dodging the footsteps of the shoppers who filled the streets again. As she approached the park and slipped under the black iron gate, she heard a familiar voice calling her.

"Nicole! Nicole! Over here, dear." It was Mrs. Applejohn, still dragging her young Rupert by the sleeve.

"Rupert has something to tell you," she said, pushing her son in front of her. "Well, go on. Tell her what you told me."

Rupert stood there staring at his feet. He looked up at Nicole and then back down to his feet.

"Is it about the twins?" asked Nicole.

Rupert nodded solemnly.

"Do you know where they are?" Nicole was trying to remain calm.

Rupert looked at his mother. "Go on," she said.

In the tiniest of voices he began. "We were pretending that we were fighting mean ol' alley cats. They were real big and tough but we were beating 'em real good. Then old Mr. Dumble called us over to the rock where he was sitting." Rupert's voice grew more excited as he spoke. "He told us about a place where they have the biggest and meanest ol' cats in the world! And if a mouse could beat one of these cats he would be the bravest mouse ever! So me and the twins..."

"The twins and I, dear..." interrupted

Mrs. Applejohn.

"The twins and I," continued Rupert, "decided we were going to go and find one 'cause we know we could beat any ol' cat!"

Nicole's eyes grew large. "Where did Mr. Dumble say this place is? Is it around here?"

"Sure," answered Rupert. "I was going to go too, but . . ."

"But I grabbed him when the rain started," said Mrs. Applejohn. "Thank my lucky stars! I hate to think what might have happened to my baby if . . ."

"But where did they go, Rupert?" Nicole asked sternly.

Rupert looked up at his mother. Then he turned back to Nicole. He hung his head and said, in a whisper, "The Wild-berry Lot."

"The Wild-berry Lot?" gasped Nicole.

"Now don't worry, dear," said Mrs. Applejohn as she reached down to put her arms around her safe little boy. "Surely they wouldn't really go to the Wild-berry Lot. You know how kids love to pretend. Why only yesterday I was talking to Mrs. Doorchester about her son Otis and she said . . ." But when she looked up, Nicole was already running down the street. "Dear, you're not

17

going to that dreadful place alone, are you?"
called Mrs. Applejohn.

Nicole was already too far away to hear.

All the city mice knew about the Wildberry Lot. Old mice would speak in hushed tones as they retold stories of one or another mouse (whom they had known personally) who had gone to the dreaded place never to be heard from again. Youngsters would squirm in delicious fright as their older brothers and sisters made up scary tales about the Wildberry Lot and the terrible Wileycats.

Wileycats, it seemed, had once been ordinary alley cats. But after they took a bite of the dark purple wild-berries that grew all over the lot, they became fierce and vicious monsters. Although it seemed no one had actually seen one, the Wileycats were said to be twice the size of a normal cat, with claws that were long and sharp as knives. Their eyes were bright yellow and their fur was as purple as the berries they ate. But those same berries that turned tame little cats into wild and ferocious creatures, were said to be deadly poison to a mouse. One bite of the delicious wild-berry meant instant death! Unless, of course, you were a cat.

Not everyone believed the legend. Some of the younger mice scoffed when old-timers related these tales they heard as children. But even those who didn't believe, managed to go blocks out of their way rather than pass near the lot. Once in a great while a daring young mouse would venture into the wilderness of the Wild-berry Lot. Not one had ever returned.

❧ ❧ ❧

Nicole rounded the corner into the street leading to the Wild-berry Lot. Her heart pounded. She stopped to catch her breath. She had never strayed this far from the loft. The farthest she had ever gone before was to Clacker Street, and that was just a quick trip to pick up a piece of marvelous blue plush velvet that a friend of the major's had spotted on his way home from the docks. He would have brought it to her himself, he had explained, had he not been already loaded down with a hefty chunk of bleu cheese, fresh off the boat. Now Nicole stood staring across the street at the green leaves that spilled over

19

onto the sidewalk.

She waited until there were no trucks coming and scampered over to the edge of the lot. Green bushes seemed to be everywhere; bright and glistening in the sunlight, dark and mysterious in the shadows. The leaves were dotted with purple berries that, from a distance, looked just like thousands of shiny black buttons. A network of tiny trails criss-crossed around and under the wild-berry bushes leading to secret places. It would be impossible to imagine what terrible things took place within that leafy jungle known as the Wild-berry Lot; but one brave little French mouse was about to find out.

૪ૡ ૪ૡ ૪ૡ

Nicole found a small opening and what appeared to be the beginning of a trail. On each side of the trail hung the bright green leaves and the dark purple berries . . . berries that could kill a hungry mouse the moment one was eaten. She looked at the plump berries and shuddered. They had a delicious aroma which made them seem even more dangerous.

Nicole tore a small corner off her croissant

roll and put it in her mouth. She hadn't eaten since morning and would need all her energy for what lay ahead. Studying the path she was about to take, she tried not to think of the frightening stories she had heard. The only thing that mattered was to find the twins. She took one deep breath and ducked into the tangle of branches overhanging the path.

The trail twisted and turned, leading her down one hill and up the next. She could hear distant fog horns from the ships and the roar of trucks rattling through the streets. As she wandered deeper and deeper into the damp confusion of leaves, the sounds faded and it became quiet. She leaped over a tiny river of rain water and found herself at the end of the trail. On all sides there were nothing but dark green leaves, twisting branches and purple berries. She heard only the wind and the sound of her own heart beating. She looked around her. It was silly, she thought, for a trail to come so far and then just stop. She was about to turn back when something caught her eye. Near her feet was a small patch of red that peeked through a jumble of twigs and leaves. Reaching down, she uncovered a red cap; the very cap she had knitted

for one of the twins! Searching farther, she discovered an opening through the underbrush. An opening just big enough for two small mice to crawl through, or one large one. Quickly she put the cap in her bag and crawled under the branches, being careful not to snag her plaid coat or her red neckscarf. On the other side was a clearing. The path was wider now, continuing over a small ridge just ahead.

Nicole stood up and brushed off her coat. A feeling that she wasn't alone came over her. For the first time since entering the Wild-berry Lot she was afraid. Her large dark eyes searched all around her but found nothing unusual. Still, she knew she was being watched. She was startled by a rustling of branches behind her and spun around to find it was only a gust of wind. But as she turned again toward the trail her heart jumped and her mouth fell open! There, on the very ridge that was empty only seconds before, stood three terrifying figures staring down at her!

II ❧ THE ROQUEFORT GANG

The mouse on the left was large, round, and rough-looking, wearing a ragged red and white striped sweater. Around his waist was a broad leather belt that held a bright shining sword. The mouse on the right was tall and thin. He wore a long gray overcoat that hung to his feet. The rim of his gray fedora was pulled over his eyes and a broken toothpick dangled from his mouth. He too wore a belt with a sword.

In the center stood a third mouse. He was not as big as the others but looked every bit as tough. He was dressed in an old blue military jacket. Most of the gold buttons were missing and some of the gold bands around the sleeves had been ripped off, leaving strips of darker blue. The cloth itself was worn away in several places. His wide black belt held a gleaming sword just like the others'. He stood with his feet spread apart and his arms folded on his chest. Thatches of cat fur hung like trophies from the belt of each mouse. Orange fur, gray fur, white fur, and black fur. The three young mice stood together staring down at Nicole.

Never had she seen such a sight! They certainly didn't dress like respectable mice! But Nicole was no longer afraid. There was something about these three mice, who dressed so strangely and looked so tough, that made her feel safe. She sensed that they might even be friendly.

It was the young mouse in the middle who finally broke the silence. Without taking his eyes off Nicole, he shuffled sideways down from the ridge to the clearing where she stood. Slowly, he walked around her in a complete circle, as if trying to figure out what a young, innocent-looking mouse was doing here in the center of the dreaded Wild-berry Lot. He stopped suddenly, directly in front of her, and demanded, "Do you realize where you are?"

"The Wild-berry Lot," she said.

"And I suppose you've heard of the Wileycats?" He looked at her from the corner of his eye, waiting for her reaction.

"Of course," she answered seriously. "I have been very fortunate not to have run into one! You know, you and your friends had better be careful. There's no way to escape from those vicious creatures! They'd just as soon eat you as look at you! They're always waiting for strange mice to wander by."

The large mouse on the left started to laugh but quickly controlled himself. "We're not strange mice," he blurted out. "We live here!"

Nicole was astonished. "You live here? What about the Wileycats?"

The young mouse in front of her patted a clump of jet-black fur that hung from his belt. "See this? It once belonged to the biggest and meanest alley cat you'd ever want to meet. Somehow I don't think he'll be back to bother us! And the same goes for the others!" All three mice pointed proudly to their prizes.

Nicole shivered. "As terrible as cats may be, I never approve of killing . . ."

"Oh, we don't kill them," he continued. "We just teach them a lesson." He drew his sword and slashed the air for emphasis. "And when they're turning to run away we whack off some fur from their tails for a souvenir. They're so humiliated that they don't dare show their faces here again!"

"That explains the alley cats, but what about the Wileycats?" she asked again.

"The Wileycats?" he answered. "I'm afraid we've never met one."

Again the large round mouse on the ridge had to keep himself from laughing.

Nicole was becoming impatient. If they lived here as they said they did, why had they never met a Wileycat? And what did the mouse in the striped sweater find so amusing whenever she asked a simple question? She was beginning to feel as if a joke was being played on her. "Just who are you, anyway?" she asked.

As if on cue, the two on the ridge jumped down to join their friend. As one, they drew their swords and thrust them skyward, shiny tips meeting overhead. Together they chanted:

"We're three for one
and one for three.
The Roquefort Gang
is who are we!
Though danger's near

we think not twice.
What's there to fear?
ARE WE NOT MICE?"

They finished their song and brought their swords down smartly. With a flourish they slid them back into their belts. The mouse in the middle spoke again.

"This is Giovanni," he said, cocking his head toward the large mouse in red and white. Giovanni sucked in his stomach and tugged at his sweater as if trying to get rid of the wrinkles. His immense size and his shaggy fur made him a fearsome sight. But Nicole sensed no meanness. In fact, he seemed quite pleasant.

"Pleased to meet . . ." He broke off suddenly. Clearing his throat, he started over, this time in a lower voice. "Pleased to meet you," he said.

"And this is Sid," continued the middle mouse, motioning to his tall friend in the overcoat and fedora.

Sid stood motionless, except for the toothpick flicking from one side of his mouth to the other side, and said, without smiling, "Charmed."

Nicole turned back to the mouse in the

tattered blue military jacket.

"And I'm Marlowe," he said.

Although his coat was threadbare and his ruddy brown fur quite disheveled, she rather liked the way he looked. Dressed in a fine camel's-hair coat, she imagined, he would be handsome indeed.

"We live here," he continued, "and nobody tells us what to do. We're just after adventure! When we're hungry we take what we need." As he said this he drew his sword and deftly pierced the croissant sticking out of Nicole's bag. He lifted it into the air and

with a quick turn of the wrist, withdrew the sword, letting the roll fall back into the bag. It happened so quickly that Nicole had no time to be surprised or afraid.

"You mean you don't pay for your food?" she asked. "What would your families say if they knew?"

"We don't have real families. But we don't need 'em," said Marlowe, matter-of-factly. "We've made our own family . . . the Roquefort Gang! And we make our own rules!" The three stood closer together in a defiant pose.

"Still, it's not right to take something and not leave something in return," Nicole persisted.

Marlowe could easily handle mean and hungry alley cats. All you had to do was outsmart them and chop a chunk of fur from their tails and they wouldn't be back. But here was a young girl mouse wearing a simple green and blue plaid coat, speaking with a French accent, telling him what he should and should not do! He spoke again.

"We get our food in our own way. But I think you had better tell us who you are and what you're doing here on our lot."

Giovanni imitated Marlowe's serious attitude. Sid chewed on his toothpick.

Nicole told them her name and her story. She told them how Mrs. Applejohn had forgotten to watch the twins, and how young Rupert had mentioned the Wild-berry Lot, and how she had found the very cap she had knitted for one of the twins, just minutes ago, lying in the underbrush. Now, she said, she was afraid the Wileycats might find the twins before she did! As she finished speaking she realized again the danger that threatened the twins, and large tears appeared in her eyes. But she wouldn't let herself cry and wiped the tears away with her sleeve.

"You don't have to worry about Wileycats," Marlowe assured her. "There's no such thing."

Nicole was shocked! "You are sure?"

"Sure I'm sure! Just because mice who came to the Wild-berry Lot were never seen again, everyone thought that there were horrible monsters who gobbled them up." He curled his fingers, monster-like, above his head as he spoke. "Since nobody knew what really happened, they believed the worst. Before you knew it, they had given the creatures a name and even knew what one looked like. Do you know anyone who has ever *seen* a Wileycat?"

Nicole shook her head, "No . . . but I've heard . . ."

"Ha!" laughed Marlowe. "You've heard, I've heard, everybody's heard! But nobody's seen! Nobody's seen one because there *are* none! I'll tell you why no mice ever return from here. It's because of the bla . . ."

But he was interrupted by Nicole.

"Oh, no!" she cried.

While Marlowe had been talking, Giovanni had reached over to a branch covered with deadly wild-berries, had calmly picked one, and taken a large bite.

"Do something quickly! He'll be poisoned and die!" Nicole dropped her bag and ran toward Giovanni.

Giovanni looked surprised and stopped chewing. With a loud gulp, he swallowed. He turned, looked helplessly at his two friends, and spun around in a circle. He flopped over on his back, his big feet flying into the air then falling with a thud. A shiver ran through his body. His eyes stared blankly as dark wild-berry juice trickled from the corner of his mouth. Suddenly he sat stiffly upright, saluted his fellow gang members goodbye, and flopped again to the ground. This time he did not move.

In an instant Nicole was kneeling over the still body. "Hurry," she cried, "get some water! We must do something!"

She put her head to his chest and listened for a heartbeat, but heard nothing. As she pressed her ear closer, the huge chest slowly began to move. Then it was heaving up and down, and she realized the "corpse" was shaking with laughter! She looked up and saw Marlowe and Sid doubled over, trying to hold back. Soon the three gang members were rolling on the ground, weak with laughter.

Nicole was humiliated. She stood up angrily, threw her bag over her shoulder, and turned toward the ridge.

"We were only joking," called Marlowe. "Don't go. Maybe we can help."

Nicole paused. "I'm sure I will do just as well by myself!" she snapped. "I certainly wouldn't want to keep you children from playing your silly games, with your silly clothes and your silly swords!"

As she started down the other side of the

ridge, her foot caught on a wild root stretched across the path and she fell, head over heels, down the little hill. Her bag spilled open, the croissant flying one way, the cheese another, and pieces of string everywhere. Marlowe, Giovanni and Sid ran to the edge of the ridge, sobered by her sudden misfortune.

Marlowe slid, feet first, down the hill to where she had fallen. He began picking up string but she grabbed it out of his hand and said, "I assure you, Mr. Marlowe, that I do not need any help from you or your Gang!" She picked up all of the string and what was left of the croissant roll and started down the trail in a huff.

She was already out of sight when Marlowe called, "Watch out for the black box!" He was not sure she had heard him.

The three mice stood there feeling ashamed of the joke they had played on Nicole.

"Let's go back to the hideout," said Giovanni, softly. "It's almost dinnertime."

Marlowe was still looking down the path Nicole had taken. "You guys go. I'm not very hungry. Think I'll climb up to Water Can Hill."

Giovanni and Sid left him standing alone.

35

※ ※ ※

Water Can Hill was the highest point on the Lot. Marlowe followed a steep wandering trail until he reached an old water can. By crawling through the rusted-out hole in its side and climbing up into the look-out spout, one could see the entire Wild-berry Lot. Marlowe thought it was the loveliest view he had ever seen, especially at this hour when the sun was beginning to set.

He often came here when he was troubled or when he just wanted to think. Tonight he thought about Nicole. He liked her very much, but for some reason everything had gone wrong. He had wanted to help her but ended up hurting her feelings. Now he was uneasy. She could be in great danger!

The light was fading as he searched for a sign of Nicole. At last he thought he spotted her on the far side of the lot, near the alley. Then he saw something that gave him a start! He leaped from the look-out spout and flew down the hill, half running, half falling. He raced through the twisting trail toward the hideout. He had to get the others. Nicole was in trouble!

III ❧ THE BLACK BOX

Nicole made her way through the thick Wild-berry jungle feeling angry, frustrated and hurt. She had heard Marlowe calling to her as she ran, but did not know what he had said. *Not that she cared!* She would find the twins by herself. The discovery of the red knitted cap proved that she was on the right trail, and now that there were no Wileycats to look out for, what was to stop her?

Patches of purple sky peeked through the maze of branches and leaves above her, and the first stars of the evening appeared before a dark, swirling cloud blotted them out again. Continuing at a steady pace, she came upon a clearing and stopped to look around. She had reached the far side of the Wild-berry Lot! But she still had not found the twins. Now she was confused. This might be a good time,

she decided, to rest and think of what to do next.

Nicole found the remains of her croissant, blew a speck of dirt from it, and looked for a comfortable place to sit down. She noticed a smooth black metal box not far from where she stood. She walked over and, using her bag as a cushion, sat down and leaned back against the shiny box. As she nibbled at her bread, she was suddenly overtaken by a powerful and familiar smell; the smell of fresh cheese. Camembert to be exact! Her favorite since childhood!

She knew the smell was not coming from her bag as her cheese had rolled away when she fell down the hill earlier. Besides, hers had been a rather stale mild cheddar. This was an intense aroma that had her nose sniffing for direction. She followed the smell around the corner of the black box where she discovered a doorway. Perhaps, she thought, there was a family of mice inside sitting down to supper and maybe they might ask her in to join them for a bite. She could use some good food right now, not to mention kind, sympathetic company. Cautiously, she looked inside. It was very dark but she could see that the box was empty. Empty, that is, except for a large chunk of pale yellow Camembert sitting right in the middle. She backed out of the doorway and examined the strange box. It gave her a disturbed feeling. And yet, it seemed safe enough. There was nobody around and she was becoming more and more aware of just how hungry she really was.

Peering into the box again, she finally decided. She would go in, quickly tear off a chunk of cheese and bring it right back outside to eat. She still sensed danger, but the temptation of the delicious cheese was overpowering.

She selected a proper length of lightweight, but strong, kite string to leave as payment for her meal and stepped through the opening. The cold dark box gave her the creeps! She decided to hurry. She laid the string on the floor, next to the cheese, and then reached to break off a piece. At the very instant her hand met the cheese, a heavy spring snapped, and a door of metal bars slammed down over the opening!

Nicole was terrified! She ran to the door and tried to push it open but it was too strong. She ran from wall to wall, frantically feeling for a way out. There were bars all around her. The black box had concealed a cage and she was trapped inside! She cried out for help. There was no answer.

For the first time in her life Nicole felt completely alone. Even when she crossed the ocean from her home in France she was not alone. She had shared a luxurious cabin with the captain of the ship, sleeping in the drawer where the captain stored his linen handkerchiefs and white dress shirts, and eating the last morsels of food he left on his plate each night before retiring. She was certain he had left the food just for her because she'd polished the brass buttons on his coat each night in return. On the last night of the voyage she had placed a colorful bottle cap in the pocket of each shirt to show her appreciation. She knew the captain would be delighted when he discovered them!

But now she felt as if she had no one. And, what was worse, she felt she had let down the twins by allowing herself to get trapped. How welcome the sight of the Roquefort Gang would be now. They really didn't seem so bad, after all. They had offered to help. Now she wished she had accepted.

There was nothing to do but wait. She pulled her coat tightly around her and snuggled in a corner, trying to keep warm. Tears trembled from her eyes and slid down her soft golden cheeks. She was alone, afraid, and completely exhausted. In a moment she was asleep.

❧ ❧ ❧

The Roquefort Gang's hideout was a large wooden crate half buried in the ground. The crate, which originally had held ginger root from Hong Kong, still had a faint pleasant odor about it. It was divided in half by a thin wall of wood, and the three mice had added more partitions so that each enjoyed his own room. Hidden under a bush, its location was known only to the gang. At present, the hideout was a clatter of activity. Always eager for excitement, the three mice scurried about, preparing for the coming adventure.

Sid sharpened the blade of his sword with a piece of emery cloth. His sword, like Marlowe's and Giovanni's, was a large upholstery needle. The eye of the needle made an excellent handle and the tip stayed very sharp. Giovanni ransacked the kitchen, making sure there would be plenty to eat on the journey. Cheese, crackers, part of a doughnut, and a few berries . . . . he was trying to decide what to leave behind as it all would not fit into his backpack.

Marlowe rummaged through a large chest, formerly a box of kitchen matches, pulling out safety pins, bobby pins, straight pins, matches, a plastic toothpick; anything might be useful in an emergency. He placed these into a bag that he slung over his shoulder.

Finally they were ready. All three checked their belts and swords and came together in the center of the room. The light from a candle danced on their faces. Marlowe looked at the other two. Giovanni stood ready, his hand resting on the handle of his sword. Sid stood motionless, except for the toothpick he chewed. They formed a small circle.

Marlowe spoke quietly: "Three for one and one for three."

"Three for one and one for three," Giovanni and Sid answered.

Then all three shouted, "THREE FOR ONE AND ONE FOR THREE!"

Marlowe snuffed out the candle and they headed into the darkness.

❧ ❧ ❧

Three silhouettes stole silently across the lot. They reached the ridge where they had met Nicole and continued down the tiny trail in the direction of the black box. Suddenly, Marlowe signaled the others to halt. He had keen ears and was sure he heard a cat on the prowl nearby. They waited, hands on swords. Sure enough, a scraggly old orange and white tabby wandered across the path directly in front of them. They were not afraid of the cat, but now was no time for a confrontation. The cat disappeared slowly into the brush and the Roquefort Gang continued.

They arrived at the clearing, and there was the black box, sitting in evil silence. A bright, full moon, which had just appeared through a hole in the turbulent clouds, cast an eerie light over the box, causing the three to shudder.

"Wait here," said Marlowe. "I'm going to see if Nicole's all right. Warn me if someone comes."

Giovanni and Sid hid behind a fat twig while Marlowe darted across the moonlit clearing to the black box. He found the barred doorway and peeked inside. It was very dark, but he could just make out Nicole's form huddled in a far corner. He was about to call her name when a loud whistle pierced the air. The whistle was Giovanni's and it meant danger. Marlowe ran to peer around the corner of the box and saw two headlights speeding towards him up the alley. One lit up the road in front of the car, the other shot off aimlessly toward the sky. Marlowe knew the car. It was what they expected.

There was no time to warn Nicole. Marlowe ran quickly to the twig that hid Giovanni and Sid, sprinted over it, and took a position between the two, not saying a word.

They watched a dilapidated dark car roll up to the curb, a few feet in front of them. A large man, dressed in a navy pea coat and rumpled black pants, got out and crossed in front of the headlights toward the lot. He picked up the box containing Nicole and set another, just like it, in its place.

While the man was making the switch, Marlowe, Giovanni and Sid took off toward the beat-up sedan. They leaped, one at a time, from the curb onto the rear bumper and clambered up behind the license plate. They held on tight, expecting a rough ride.

The license plate light blinked on and off as the idling car sputtered, making the three mice flicker like an old-time movie. Braced and ready to go, they heard the man climb back in the car and slam the door. With a roar of the engine and a cloud of exhaust fumes, they were off!

Tires squealed as the car skidded around deserted corners. The three mice hung on. The wind snapped at their neck scarves and pinned their ears to the sides of their heads. It threatened to blow off Sid's hat and he reached to save it. As the car swerved, Sid lost his grip and started to sail away into the night. Marlowe quickly grabbed Sid's hand but lost his own grip in the process. In the same instant, Giovanni grabbed Marlowe's free hand while still holding fast to the license plate. It looked like a game of crack-the-whip as Marlowe and Sid flapped in the wind, while Giovanni held on with all his strength and gradually pulled them to safety. Back behind the license plate, they held on more tightly than ever.

The car came to a screeching halt in front of an old desolate building. A lone street light shone down on the building as a thick carpet of fog crawled up the street. The air was chilly and smelled of sea water.

The three mice jumped from the bumper. They quickly shook out their bodies, jostled from the ride, and ran for the doorway of the building. The man climbed out of the car carrying the black box under his arm. He stopped in the shadow of the doorway and pulled a ring of keys from his pocket. Sid took the opportunity to climb into one of the man's pants cuffs and Giovanni, with a leg-up from Marlowe, pulled himself into the other. But before Marlowe could do the same, the man had opened the door and was walking down a

cold, dark hallway with a strong odor of mildew. Marlowe hurried behind, deftly side-stepping chunks of wall plaster and rotted moulding that littered the floor. The man descended a stairway leading to a cellar. As Marlowe followed in the darkness, he stumbled over a piece of plaster and tumbled into a pile of empty bottles.

The clamor brought the man flying back up the stairs. He pulled a flashlight from his coat pocket. Marlowe dove under a scrap of newspaper as a dim shaft of light swept across the floor. The weak yellow beam searched among the bottles and came to rest on the very paper that hid Marlowe. He dared not move a whisker!

Finding no movement, the man reluctantly put the flashlight back into his pocket and continued down the stairs. Marlowe immediately resumed the chase. As another door opened, Marlowe shot between the man's boots into a darkened room and slipped behind the first large object he bumped into.

The man pulled a light chain hanging from an overhead rafter: the room filled with a harsh white glare. Marlowe found himself behind the leg of a wooden table, inches from where the man stood. It was not a good hiding place. Sid and Giovanni peeked out from the man's pants cuffs and were shocked to see their pal standing right next to them. How had he gotten into the room before they did? But there was no time for questions now.

Quickly and quietly Giovanni and Sid let themselves down from the cuffs. Then all three ran behind a stack of boxes sitting against the wall. They watched as the man set the black box on the table, opened the lid, and pulled out the snug-fitting cage. He banged the cage down on the table. Marlowe was relieved to see that Nicole was unhurt, though it was obvious that she was frightened. Her dark eyes darted fearfully about the room.

The man pulled off his heavy jacket and threw it over the back of a chair. He picked up the empty black box and took it into an adjoining room, leaving the cage and its prisoner on the table.

As the door closed, the three mice crossed the room to the chair, climbed up a sleeve of the man's coat, and made a short hop to the table top.

"Don't worry," said Marlowe, "we'll get you out of here!"

Nicole had never been so happy to see anyone in her life! She was much too surprised to speak.

"When we pry open the door," he instructed, "you jump out in a hurry. I don't know how long we can hold it."

Giovanni, being the biggest, grabbed the bottom of the cage door and pulled hard. His body shook as he strained every muscle. Gradually, a small space appeared below the door. Sid and Marlowe quickly slid matchsticks into the space. With the matchsticks in position they pried the door open wider, and Giovanni, now able to get better leverage, forced the door up allowing the others to reposition the matchsticks, placing them on end. One slight bump would cause the matchsticks to snap and the door to come crashing down with enough force to break the bones of even the largest mouse!

"You can come out now," said Marlowe. "Be careful not to touch the matchsticks."

Nicole held her bag close to her body and slipped under the door with room to spare. She was free! The four mice greeted each other as if they were old friends. They were about to climb down from the table when they heard two small voices calling.

"Nicole, Nicole! We're up here!"

Nicole and her three friends turned and saw what they had been too busy to notice before. Against the opposite wall were stacks and stacks of large cages filled with mice. The captives were staring at Nicole and the three strange tough-looking mice who had just rescued her. They sat in their cages, sad-eyed and silent. But in a cage that had been placed high on top of the others, she saw two little mice waving and calling her name!

"The twins!" cried Nicole.

"Get us out of here, Nicole," they called. "We want to go home!"

"Are you all right?" she called back.

"We're hungry," answered one.

"They want to feed us to snakes!" added the other.

Nicole gasped.

"That's right," said a gray, droopy-cheeked old timer in the cage under the twins. "We're all gonna end up in a laboratory as guinea pigs for some scientific experiment. Either that or in some boa's belly. Yup, the next shipment goes out tomorrow."

Nicole was horrified. She had heard of mice being kidnapped and shipped all over the world to be sacrificed for scientific research, but she had never really believed it.

She wheeled around to ask Marlowe what they were to do and, in her excitement, accidentally swung her bag into one of the matchsticks holding the cage door open. The door came down with a mighty clang!

Marlowe knew the man must have heard the noise and would be there in an instant. He grabbed Nicole by the sleeve and pulled her after him, down the table leg, across the floor, and behind the boxes where Giovanni and Sid were already hidden.

The man banged through the door. He spotted the empty cage and let out a snarl.

"So you think you can get away, do you?" he growled. "We'll just see about that!" He turned back into the adjoining room. The mice stood frozen behind the boxes, their hearts beating fast. Nicole looked nervously at Marlowe. He put his hand on hers.

"Don't you worry," he whispered, "we're ready for anything."

Giovanni nodded in agreement. Sid chewed nonchalantly on his toothpick.

Then the door slammed shut and they heard a deep voice from within the room.

"Where are you, my little darlings?" it purred.

It was a chilling voice. The gang members looked at each other with wide eyes. Cautiously, they peeked around the edge of a box and beheld the largest cat they had ever seen. Pacing slowly around the room, he spoke again, in a low hiss:

"Come to me, my little sweets,
You mustn't hide from your Uncle
Keats."

IV ❧ KEATS

He was big and fat and covered with extremely
long, luxuriously soft, shiny black fur. His
voice was honey-smooth. It rose and fell as
he spoke, giving his speech a hypnotic song-
like quality. He moved softly on large paws
while his yellow eyes searched about the
room. He stopped to lick his wavy fur, eyes
becoming narrow slits; then admired his
reflection as he padded slowly past a glass
bookcase. Having made a complete circle of
the room, he settled down in the center of
the floor, facing the boxes that hid the four
mice. In his most velvety voice, he said:
"Would old Keats harm you?
Don't be absurd.
I'd just like to *see* you,
I give you my word!"
Nicole and her rescuers did not move.

Marlowe was trying desperately to think of a plan. It would be fairly simple for the four mice to save themselves, but to escape with the twins would be much more difficult. The Roquefort Gang never had to think of anyone but themselves until now. They were adventurers and liked to travel fast and light. Now they were faced with the responsibility of protecting Nicole and rescuing a set of rambunctious twins, hardly more than babies! Finally, Marlowe thought of a way.

"Look," he said, "that poetic pussy-cat doesn't know how many we are. Nicole and I will distract him while you two sneak around to the cages and release the twins. Here, take this in case you need it." He slid the bag of pins and sticks off his back and handed it to Sid.

Giovanni gave Marlowe the thumbs-up sign. Sid shifted the toothpick in his mouth. Together they crept to the far side of the boxes. Marlowe turned to Nicole.

"This is gonna take some nerve," he said. "Just do as I do."

Nicole looked straight at him. "I'm not afraid," she answered.

"Good," he said, taking her hand, "'cause

here we go!"

He led her around to the edge of the box. He leaned his head out and called loudly: "Hey, Keats!"

Keats' eyes shot to the edge of the box. His plush tail began flicking from side to side. "Yes, my little darlings," he purred.

"We want to talk to you," said Marlowe.

"Of course. But come out and let me have a look at you," responded Keats.

"Promise not to come after us?" asked Marlowe.

"Cat's honor!" lied Keats.

Marlowe whispered into Nicole's ear, "If anything goes wrong be ready to run."

He walked cautiously out into the open, Nicole following close behind.

"Oh, my!" gushed Keats, "What a pretty couple. Wouldn't you like to come a little closer?" His tail flicked more rapidly as he spoke.

"No thanks," answered Marlowe. "Normally we would have tried to run away, but we notice that you are well-bred and educated, and display a rare gift in the arts. We are both quite fond of poetry [he smiled sweetly at Nicole] and, to be honest, we find that most

of our mouse-friends are much too ignorant
to share our appreciation. Since we know we
havn't a chance of escaping you anyway, we
wondered if you might . . . that is, if it's not
too much trouble, if you might recite one of
your poems for us."

"Oh yes, please do, please do!" joined in
Nicole. "We know you must have a great
masterpiece somewhere."

Keats was very surprised. He had never
known mice to be so intelligent and percep-
tive. "Well, maybe just a short one," he said.
"Perhaps I'll make up a couplet for you."

"No, no!" cried Marlowe. "Give us your best. Before you eat us we want to hear your masterpiece!"

"It will be an honor to be eaten by a great poet such as yourself," added Nicole.

Had he not been so conceited Keats might have been suspicious of such elaborate praise. Instead, he scratched his large head and searched his memory for an appropriate "masterpiece."

"I think I have just the poem for you," he said at last.

"Oh, this is so exciting," cooed Nicole as she and Marlowe sat on the floor, pretending to make themselves comfortable.

"I call it 'Poor, Poor Pussy,'" said Keats.

"Bravo, bravo!" shouted Marlowe.

"I haven't even started yet!" Keats was annoyed at the interruption.

"I know, but just the way you announced 'Poor, Poor Pussy,'" said Marlowe, doing an excellent imitation of Keats, "I was reminded of the famous French poet, Pierre La Bouche."

"Oh, no!" argued Nicole. "He's much better than Pierre La Bouche."

Keats had never heard of Pierre La Bouche but, not wanting to seem ignorant, said,

"Hmmm, certainly Pierre La Bouche is not without a certain charm, but, at the risk of sounding immodest, I think you will find my poetry to be much ... much...." He was searching for just the right word " ... BETTER!" was all he could say.

"Hear, hear!" agreed Marlowe. He and Nicole settled back, appearing to be thoroughly engrossed.

✿ ✿ ✿

Keats stood up, one paw placed over his heart and the other held aloft as if warding off an invisible storm. He cleared his throat. When the room was perfectly quiet, he began:
"Poor, poor pussy
So frightened and alone.
No porridge in your bowl,
Not one fish bone ..."
Keats was already absorbed in his own performance. Much too absorbed to notice Sid and Giovanni sneaking along the concrete wall, past the door, to the cages leaning against the wall behind him. They climbed from cage to cage toward the twins. Each cage they passed was filled with sad mice, young and old, large and small. Mice who had

given up any hope of escape but were watching with increased interest as Nicole and the Roquefort Gang proceeded with their daring plan.

Keats droned on. Nicole and Marlowe stifled yawns. They forced themselves to look alert. Not that it mattered. The big fluffy cat was so taken with his own voice that he seemed to be in a trance.

Marlowe's eyes drifted past Keats to the cages. He could see Giovanni and Sid making their way to the top, closer and closer to the twins. Suddenly, he noticed a movement up near the ceiling, directly over Keats' head. He thought he was seeing things. There, balancing himself on a rafter, was an old round military mouse with white whiskers. He was dressed in a splendid white uniform with scarlet trim. Gold braid hung in circles from his shoulders, and medals covered his chest. From a polished black belt hung a golden sword encased in a white scabbard.

Marlowe nudged Nicole with his elbow and lifted his eyes toward the ceiling. Nicole glanced up and gasped! She was about to cry, "Major Tybo!" but Marlowe quickly covered her mouth with his hand. The major saw

Nicole and waved at her, almost losing his footing on the narrow beam. Nicole looked at him as if to say "How did you get in here?" Understanding her gesture, he pointed back toward a high window that opened to the sidewalk in front of the building. Then he placed his hand on his sword, indicating that he was about to save the day.

Keats realized that he had lost the attention of his audience. He stopped his poem in the middle of a rhyme and saw Nicole and Marlowe staring at the rafter above his head. "Is there something I should know about?" asked Keats.

"Oh, no," replied Marlowe. "It's just easier to concentrate on the deep meaning . . ."

Before Marlowe could finish his sentence, Keats had turned and was looking at the rafter above his head. He saw Major Tybo and became furious. The major, disconcerted by the fierce look in the cat's eyes, slipped from the rafter.

Then everything happened at once! As old Major Tybo fell, he grabbed the chain hanging from the overhead light. The light blinked off and on again. Giovanni and Sid leaped down from the wall of cages and scrambled

behind the boxes. Keats began running in circles, not knowing whether to go after Nicole
and Marlowe or wait for the fat little intruder
to drop from the light chain. The major made
Keats' decision for him. He lost his grip on
the chain and fell.

He landed right on the bewildered cat's
nose. Keats let out a yowl, more from surprise
than pain. The major pulled at his sword but
it wouldn't come free. Keats took one swipe
with his enormous paw and knocked the
sword and scabbard flying from the major's
belt. Then he picked up the old mouse in one

paw, ready to eat him, Royal Danish Mouse Corps uniform and all!

In a second, he stopped. The major, whose eyes were shut tightly, opened them to find out why he wasn't being chewed up and swallowed. Keats leaped onto the table still holding the major in his paw. Effortlessly, he opened the door to the cage that, not long ago, had held Nicole, and tossed the little round soldier inside. Then, with a devilish smile, Keats stretched the entire length of his body and lay down on the table right in front of the cage. He called out to Marlowe and Nicole:

"It seems I've caught your friend.

Oh, dear,
And suppertime is drawing near.
I'm sure he'll make a tasty dish
If you don't do just as I wish!"

There was no response.

"I know you hear me," he hissed, looking around the room at all the places where two mice might be hiding. "You'll have to try and save your brave, but foolish, friend sometime, and I'll be waiting right here." He adjusted his oversized body to a more comfortable position as he lay guarding the cage.

꩜ ꩜ ꩜

Marlowe, Nicole, Giovanni, and Sid reassembled behind the familiar stack of boxes. Knowing that this would be the first place Keats would think to look for them, they climbed to the shelf above and shinnied up an electrical cord connected to an old radio sitting on a shelf much higher up. They were out of breath from the climb as they grouped together behind the radio. The gang members were impressed that Nicole was able to keep up with them. She told them it was her daily ballet exercises that kept her so fit.

They gazed down from their high vantage point and saw Keats waiting and watching. Poor, helpless Major Tybo, stripped of his magnificent golden sword, sat in a corner of the cage.

Marlowe, Giovanni and Sid began to discuss their next move. It seemed that the only chance left now was to confront the powerful Keats in a head-to-head battle. Nicole kept looking down on the large cat. She watched Keats stretch his front paws and give in to a mighty yawn. His big yellow eyes gradually grew narrow, almost closing. With a jerk of his head he quickly popped them open again. Nicole realized that Keats was dozing. It was getting late and the lazy old cat was probably up far past his bedtime. This gave her an idea.

She raced behind the radio where the others were preparing for a terrible fight with Keats. A fight they knew they might lose.

"Maybe we won't need to fight him after all," said Nicole, excitedly. "I think I have a plan!"

She dumped all the string out of her bag and started Marlowe, Giovanni and Sid tying the pieces together, end to end, to form one long length. While they were doing this, Nicole leaned over the edge of the high shelf and began to sing. It was a delightful French lullaby she had learned from her grandmother as a child. When Keats heard the melody he snapped his head up and looked right at her.

"Ah-ha! I knew where you were all along." he bragged. Then, in a low honeyed tone, he said:

"Come, save your foolish major fast
Or my next meal will be his last!"

Extremely proud of his latest rhyme, Keats gave a smug grin and rearranged himself more solidly in front of the cage. He knew they would have to get by him if they wanted to save the major. He would be waiting for them. Mice were so stupidly loyal, he thought.

Nicole kept right on singing. Keats hated to admit it but she really did have a pleasant voice. It was soft and pure and had a relaxing effect on him. Soon, his eyes began to close and he blinked them back open. Gradually they closed again. This time he had to shake his head to keep himself awake. Finally, he could resist no longer. As Nicole started another verse, Keats' whole body went limp and he fell into a deep, peaceful sleep.

She let her voice trail off to nothing, then got up and ran behind the radio. There were her three rescuers as sound asleep as she had left Keats! It had been a long day for them, too. She nudged them, gently.

V ❧ THE ESCAPE

In a flash they were on their feet. They rolled up the long length of string and tossed it to the floor. Then they slid down the electrical cord as far as it went, dropped one by one to the floor, raced over to the string, and carried it to the table. Marlowe took one end and climbed up the man's coat once again, to the top of the chair. He jumped to the table, dragging the string toward Keats. The cat's huge body rose and fell with each breath. Marlowe realized now, just how big Keats was! He saw the major looking at him from the cage. Marlowe tipped an imaginary hat to him and put his finger to his lips, warning the major to remain quiet.

Slowly and carefully, Marlowe slipped the end of the string under Keats' tail, ran around to the other side, and pulled it through several inches. Then he wrapped the string around the immense tail and tied a tight knot. He considered the lone knot for a moment, then tied several more for good measure.

While Marlowe secured the string to Keats' tail, Sid, Giovanni and Nicole dragged the other end to the mouse-filled cages stacked against the wall. They passed the many-colored string in and out of the bars of selected cages on the bottom row until it reached no farther. There, Nicole tied a firm knot to the cage door.

All was set. Marlowe slid down and stationed himself with Nicole behind a table leg. Giovanni and Sid climbed to the table top and stood facing the slumbering Keats. Giovanni was nervous, so close to the large cat. Sid, who rarely had anything to say, took it upon himself to start the action.

He shouted at Keats, "Hey, Fur Ball!"

Keats jerked his head up, blinking the sleep from his eyes.

"Over here, you overgrown dust mop!" added Giovanni, bravely.

Gradually Keats began to focus his eyes. When he saw the two mice standing right in

70

front of him, a wicked smile came over his face.

"Well, well, well! What have we here?" he breathed.

"Are you the guy who tells those lousy poems?" demanded Sid.

Keats flushed with anger, but controlled himself. "Come, come," he hissed, "is that any way for a good little mouse to talk?" His tail began twitching.

"I've read better stuff on milk cartons!" said Sid, chewing on his toothpick.

"I'm warning you . . ." growled Keats, filling with rage.

"I've read better stuff on dog food labels!" blurted out Giovanni, with what he thought to be the ultimate insult to a cat.

That did it! Keats leaped to his feet and sprang toward the mice. Sid and Giovanni were astonished at how fast the big cat could move. They took off in different directions.

Keats felt something holding him. The string attached to his tail became taught and, as he lunged forward, the bottom row of cages were yanked from the wall. The cages above began to topple. One by one they crashed to the cellar floor while some of the highest ones hit the table top. The noise of crashing metal put Keats in a panic. The more he tried to run, the more cages were pulled over and the more confused he became.

Cage after cage broke open and hundreds of mice came spilling out, running in every direction. Nicole managed to find the twins' cage and pulled them free. Marlowe helped others to escape. Keats was caught in a tangle of string and, after chasing around in circles in an effort to get loose, found himself bound to a table leg. As he jostled the table with his frantic tugging, Major Tybo's cage vibrated to the table's edge. It teetered there for a moment, before falling to the floor. Gingerly, the major picked himself up and squeezed through the bars that had been bent in the collision. He ran straight for the glass bookcase and retrieved his golden sword. He refastened it to his belt and began searching for Nicole.

By now an escape route had been established, with a steady stream of happy mice running up a broom handle to the top of the bookcase and across to a water pipe that carried them to a rafter above. From there it was a short way to the window that let them out to the sidewalk.

Nicole tried to hold the twins close to her side. They were bouncing up and down with energy, enjoying their noisy rescue. Marlowe, having helped the last mouse from its cage, joined them in the center of the floor. Next, Sid and Giovanni showed up, and finally the major.

"We'd better get out of here," advised Marlowe. "That string won't hold him long."

They helped one another up the broomstick, across the bookcase, up the water pipe, and onto the rafter. As they climbed through the window, Keats broke free. Marlowe, who was the last mouse to leave, had one foot out the window when Keats called to him.

"What did you really think of my poetry?" he whined. "I've got to know."

Marlowe stopped and thought for a moment. He looked down at Keats who seemed a lot less frightening now.

"It needs work," he answered.

❧ ❧ ❧

The night was damp with fog, and the cold air turned their breathing into white puffs as they gathered under the street lamp. A noisy

73

street-sweeping machine, passing by slowly, became their transportation home. The seven mice ran along the side of the truck and grabbed the bristles of a large round brush that had momentarily stopped spinning. They quickly pulled themselves up the brush and climbed to a metal footstep below the truck's door. There they sat, side by side, their feet dangling.

As the street-sweeper rolled from curb to curb, brushes twirling, motors whirring, Nicole introduced everybody. The twins were the center of attention. They described their adventure in exaggerated detail: from the park to the Wild-berry Lot to being captured in a cold black box and taken to the cellar of cages. They interrupted each other so often, speaking and squealing at such a rapid pace, usually both at once, that Nicole had only the faintest idea of what really happened. All that mattered was that they were safe.

The major, noticing Marlowe's blue military jacket, asked which branch of service he belonged to. Marlowe answered that he was really a civilian and the major said, "Ah, yes. Undercover work! Backbone of the military."

Nicole asked the major how he happened to find the room of cages. He explained that he had wakened from his nap and read her note saying that she and the twins were going to spend the evening at Mrs. Applejohn's. But then, when Mrs. Applejohn herself came knocking at the door to inquire about the twins, he knew something was wrong. He persuaded the talkative Mrs. Applejohn to tell him what had happened that day and learned about the twins' plan to go to the Wild-berry Lot and search for Wileycats. Quickly, he had contacted his old military friends and briefed them on the situation.

Before long, information came pouring in from his sources. He learned that a young girl mouse, wearing a simple green and blue plaid coat and carrying a colorful patchwork bag, was seen entering the Wild-berry Lot. He was told a prison for mice had been discovered in the cellar of an old building near the waterfront, and that some of the mice in the prison had been trapped at the Wild-berry Lot. He put two and two together and there he was! Basic military strategy, of course.

☙ ☙ ☙

The foggy air was invigorating. As they rolled along they began to sing. The Roque-fort Gang sang a song about pirates, written by Giovanni after he'd read a rousing book on the subject. Nicole sang a *chanson* from her childhood. Then the major tried to sing his favorite Royal Danish Mouse Corps hymn. He could remember only a line here and a rhyme there, while the melody escaped him completely. He felt badly at having for-gotten; but Marlowe assured him that, had he been able to remember the words and the melody, it would have been undoubtedly the best song of the evening. Suddenly, the major felt much better.

The twins plied Giovanni and Sid with questions and were rewarded with marvelous stories of fierce cats and brave mice. Some-one mentioned that it was a wonderful night. Everybody agreed. It *was* a wonderful night!

Soon, the street-sweeper wheeled into familiar territory. Nicole spotted the bakery and everyone jumped down from the footstep of the slow-moving truck. Giovanni and Sid carried the twins, who had fallen asleep. Nicole led the way up to the loft and entered through the window. She was glad to be home again. Major Tybo went directly to his rocking chair and was snoring within a minute. Giovanni and Sid laid the twins in their beds and joined Marlowe and Nicole, who had stepped out on the roof.

It was time to say good-bye. Nicole shyly kissed each of the young adventurers on the cheek. Marlowe coughed self-consciously, Giovanni shuffled his large feet, and even Sid was a little embarrassed. "Charmed!" he said with the slightest hint of a smile.

She turned to Marlowe and said she hoped they would visit often. He promised they would, whenever they weren't involved in some dangerous adventure. Then he tore off one of the few remaining gold buttons from his jacket and gave it to her.

"If things ever get too dull around here," he offered, "you know where we live."

With that, Marlowe, Sid and Giovanni scrambled across the bakery sign, jumped to the red and blue striped awning, and scampered down the drainpipe to the street below. They turned and waved one last time. Nicole watched as they headed toward the Wildberry Lot, arms on each others' shoulders, swords swinging with each step.

As they disappeared into the darkness she could hear their voices:
    "We're three for one
      and one for three.
    The Roquefort Gang
      is who are we!
    Though danger's near
      we think not twice.
    What's there to fear?
    ARE WE NOT MICE?"